BIANCA THE BRAVE

KALEY MILLS AND KATIE CROSS
ILLUSTRATED BY LAILA SAVOLAINEN

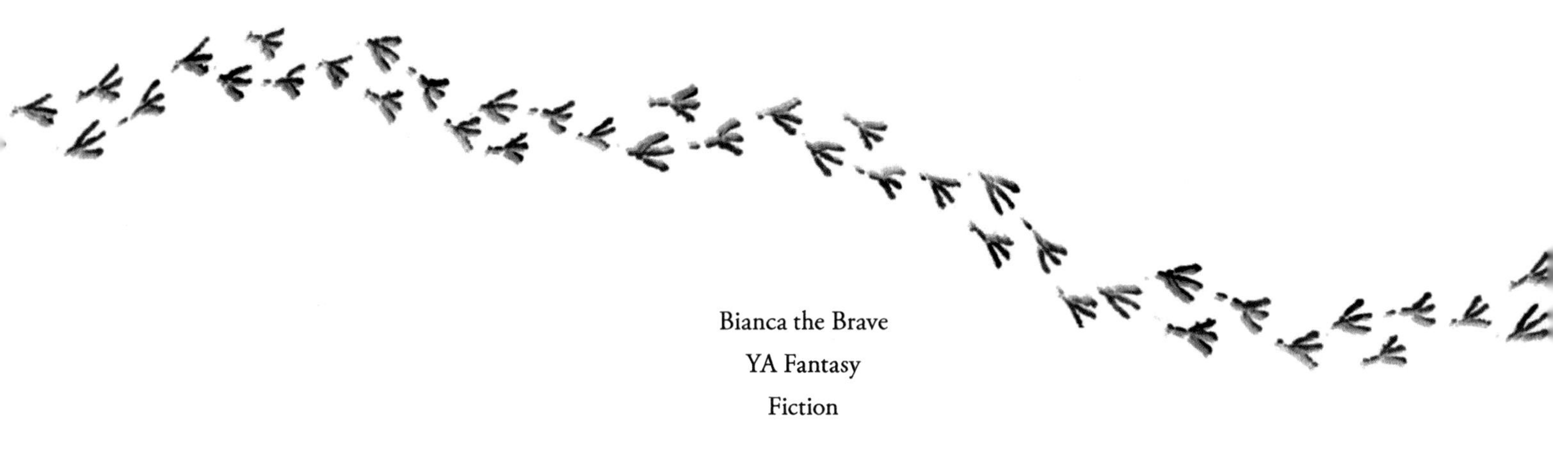

Bianca the Brave

YA Fantasy

Fiction

Illustrations by Laila Savolainen

Cover and Interior Design by Jenny Zemanek

ISBN - Hardcover: 978-1-9465088-0-5

ISBN - Paperback: 978-1-9465088-1-2

For all those who shone a light to my path, and then showed me I was worthy to walk it.

—KALEY MILLS

For all my Alkarrans.

—KATIE CROSS

Bianca Monroe was a wonder.
A sight for any and all.
She ran barefoot through the trees,
That were taller than tall.

At her side lay Viveet,
A sword glowing, shiny.
It wasn't too large,
It wasn't too tiny.

Given to her
By her Papa, no less.
He believed in them both,
As I'm sure you can guess.

In the forest they fought
The most imaginative beasts.
Together they attended
The most magical feasts.

The trees in her world,
Their voices they raised.
Forever and always,
It was her that they praised.

She cared for them deeply,
She was one with their soul.
She ran in their wild,
Legs burning like coal.

She was so used to fighting
For her home, her land,
That on the day of the fires,
She held Viveet in her hand.

The fires came fast,
Burning up trees.
Climbing their trunks,
And scorching their leaves.

With her feet firmly planted,
She faced the tall flames.
This wasn't a time,
For tricks or for games.

Thinking so quickly
Upon her two feet,
She swung Viveet wildly,
In a steady, strong beat.

The trees caught her motion,
Understood the new plan.
They started to wave,
They started to fan.

With every broad swing,
More trees joined the cue.
But Bianca Monroe
Had much more to do.

Circles and sweeps,
Loops and a blow.
The fire began to shift
To where it would go.

There just ahead
Was the river so cool.
The fire charged toward it
Like a silly old fool.

Right when she thought
All the work was complete,
She heard a small sound
Like a whimpering tweet.

As she scanned the
Inferno from bottom to top,
She noticed a tiny thing
Just trying to hop.

The little bird squeaked,
There was no hope of flying.
Bianca wouldn't have it,
This little one dying.

Sometimes a sword
Is meant for a fight.
But sometimes it's about
More than sheer might.

Bianca stopped her swinging,
Her relentless attack.
And she knelt to the ground,
With Viveet out flat.

And the fire, you ask?
What happened to it?
Swallowed by the river
In a raging loud fit!

Bianca raced on
With a solid understanding.
That sometimes the war,
needs nothing but disbanding.

Fight for your truth,
With sword in hand.
For the ones whom you love,
And of course, your land.

But lay your weapon down,
Yes, the time will arise.
When gentleness and grace
Is the choice of the wise.

KALEY MILLS

Kaley Mills never quite grew out of the kid stage!
She is a Momma to four young children , has been a teacher for over fifteen years and is one of the first female hockey coaches in her community.
She is surrounded by tiny humans!
When not reading, writing or editing, you'll find her camping in and exploring wild places in her home country of Canada with her husband and kids. Kaley is an aspiring author that has been told for years "You should write a book!"
This is her very first one.

KATIE CROSS

Katie Cross is ALL ABOUT writing epic magic and wild places.
Creating new fantasy worlds is her jam.
When she's not hiking or chasing her two littles through the Montana mountains, you can find her curled up reading a book or arguing with her husband over the best kind of sushi.

Visit her at www.katiecrossbooks.com for free short stories, extra savings on all her books (and some you can't buy on the retailers), and so much more.

This project would have been impossible without the community that backed us.
To acknowledge your contribution, you will be forever written into this book.
Thank you for supporting *Bianca the Brave*.

Aaron Mills
Lincoln Mills
Griffin Mills
Nevaya Mills
Riley Mills
Samantha Shaw
Laila Savolainen
Nicole Sanders
Jayde Abbott
Brynn Wismer
Tim Kyle
Jessi
Michelle Mason
Brittany Mills
Brittany Shearer
Alexander Mills
Mike Thompson
Sirkka Duncan
Jo Topperwien
Dave Bakker
Garrett Zeien
Kym Hulme
Denise Pratt
Steve Gossman
Kevin A. Davis
Robyn

Narelle Wynn
KJ
Kim Jones
Carol Long
Debbie Kirk
Michelle Holloway
Hazel Thompson
Andy Tolman
Amy V-H
Susan Diddle
Daniella Stukel
Erin Rowaan
Victoria L. Smith
Mary
Jason Anderson
Richard Novak
Kayla Marie
Jill Williamson
Lois Green
Lucy & Sam
Jean-Maire Cole
Jennifer
Becca Gardner
Emily Higgins
G. S. Jennsen
Suzanne Veenstra

Cindy
Evan Walter Scott Morgan
Zachary Cross
Karen J. Mueller
Monica Wilson
Beth Lobdell
Jessica Staub
Jamie Schnaak
Sherry
Abby Traverse
Jacob Moyer
Pam Shea
Damon J. Courtney
Peter Hesketh-Roberts
Kathy Shirts
Janice Hill
Meba Hart
Sharon Eastvold
Vancil Clayton
Thomas
Debbie Hill
Hill Kids (Mylie, Taysom, Parker, Mason, Cameron)
Joy Battey

Jennifer Lindley
Carol
Brooke Francom
Donn Cahill
Paula Bruce
Bee Happy Pediatrics
Bruce Chamberlain
Barbara Melton
Faith Hill
Marianne deJong
Terry Gardner
Phillip Cripe
Karen Haughn
Dakota Krout
Kevin Crowell
Andy Gonzalez de M.
Caity Sarah Falcon
Joscelin F.
Shami Stovall
Mike Shirts
Kit
Kira Wight
Diane Ottobre
Samantha Benjamin
Bradley Yandt
Mark Stallings

Mary Ellen Marino
Linda J. Wakefield
Corinne Brucks
Richard Mills
Emma St. Clair
Joel Wilstead
Steve R
Binaebi Akah Calkins
Kristen Campbell & Family
Jolynn Ward
Hailey Massie
Nikki VandenBerg
Michelle Mack
Krystyna
Andrea J.
Kevin Ikenberry
Sarah Michelle Johnson
Sushmita Srikant
Cynthia Cross
Sharon Shirley
Maria Hamlin
Morgana Best
Lisa Flower
Carl L. Johnson

John S.
Christy Romney
Andra Bohnet
Michelle Morrison
Jared Nelson
Zoie
Debbie
Nanny eDina
Jean Sylvia
Beech Rose
Sophie Z.
Michael van Koetsveld
Walter Jones
Lili Giesbrecht
Shaun Donovan
Rebecca Almanza
Whitney
Malyssa Brannon
Dixie Hickman
Chad
Tan LeBoeuf
Argyro Graphy
Bev Klassen
Becky Campitelli
Rachel Gossen
Susan Hicken
Patrick Polk
Kirsten Arthur
Andrea Wall
Erin Wilson
Elinap
Mary Ceglarski-Sherwin
Lori Branham
Mel Todd
Caitlyn Price
Heather Frederick
Brittney Willbanks
Brenda Walker
Rachel
Kerri Hilbert
Lianne Takach
Laurie Stillmaker
D. Marie
Nicolas Moyer
Kinney Family
Jeff
Greg Lamb
Ashlie
Siddoway Family
Michelle Willms
Holly
Kathy and Jeff Epp
Chris Sinclair
Bentley Searing
Gary Whitten
Elizabeth Edelheit
Kim Saylor
Rebecca Saylor
Carole Clements-Cork
Tyler O'Donnell
Roger Smith
Denise Gravano
Tony Chym
Sherry Clark
Rebecca
Rickey King
Marlena McCarthy
Ramon Terrell
Jessica Springer Guernsey
Calvin and Lucy
Amelia Voigt
Naomi Rawlings
Rafi Spitzer
Carly Arave
Heaven and Paisley Osgood
Sadie B.
Holly Flom
Carolyn Helm
Tammy Swick
Carolyn (Goose) Goossen
Colleen Feeney
Arielle Antone
Claire Ferguson-Smith
Dawn Downey
Shaughn Killeen
Wade Cooper
Jennifer Chi
Deb Marie Gilmore
Seamus Sands
Author Jamie Davis
Bryce O'Connor
Wolf Pack Pups
Devon Howard
Shelley Haines
Jennifer
Author Kel Carpenter
Jane Gilbert
Fatima Fayez
Patti DeLang
Christiana Laudie
Amy Boyles
Natasha Anne Lux
Ariel Park
Laura
David Moore
Marc
Juliana Philippa Kerrest
Melody Brave
Shawn Rose
The MacDonald Family
Connie Gray
Kathi
Erin Ross
Cora McClintock
Elizabeth Barrett
J.A. Andrews
Claude Baridon
Kristi Preston-Barnes
Lydia Sherrer
Terry S.
Kristina L. Gruell
Jayn Auge' Olinick
Nat
Ashley Cook
Michelle Burdan
Dana Donovan
Fowee Family
Ronald H. Miller
Jenna Green
Tonya Flores
Paula
Elie, Abi, Ian, and Olivia
Mary-Jo Cairns
The Calderon Medina Family
Aurore, Nerys, and Yseult Chappuis
Tom Tracy
Kathryn Jackson
Jeffrey Shabel
Kim Hannibal
Laurie Sue Cogburn
Norman Moyer
Maddie, Lucas, and Abbey
Breanna Jackson
Jennifer Grosvenor
Rose
Robin Williams
Jadee Jeanna "JJ"
Julie Metelski
Rosalie Austin
Trese
Lawrence Brady
Lorraine Kelly
Isabelle John
Brooke
Peggy Rose Leggett
Sarah Phillips
Yomara
Mamaklop50
Wendy
Felicia
Barb Chamberlain and Beth Wismer
Veronica Baranek